THE DOMINIE WORLD OF
OCEAN LIFE

ANTARCTICA

Dolphins

WRITTEN & PHOTOGRAPHED
BY KIM WESTERSKOV, Ph.D.

Dominie Press, Inc.

Introducing Dolphins

What's so special about dolphins? Why do we like them so much? I'm not really sure. There is a sense of mystery about dolphins. Some reasons for liking them might be their speed and grace, and the way they love to play. It could be how beautifully they are adapted to their oceanic life. It could be their freedom to come and go as they please, or the way they look after their young and each other.

Maybe it is also that many people see dolphins the way we would like to see *ourselves*: free, friendly, fun, energetic, peaceful, and helpful. In fact, there are many true stories about dolphins coming to the rescue when humans need their help. There is a strong dolphin/human connection.

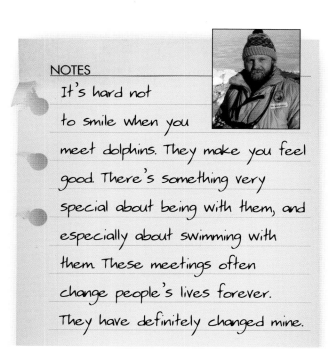

NOTES

It's hard not to smile when you meet dolphins. They make you feel good. There's something very special about being with them, and especially about swimming with them. These meetings often change people's lives forever. They have definitely changed mine.

◄ *Dusky dolphins are very acrobatic. Their leaps and tail slaps are used to show "I've found fish!" and to herd the fish.*

A common dolphin's streamlined shape helps it swim fast. ▲

2

What Is a Dolphin?

Dolphins are **mammals.** Like us, they are warm-blooded and they breathe air. The mothers give birth to live young, which they feed with their own milk. They are excellent, fast, and agile swimmers. Dolphins cruise slowly when they are not in a hurry, but some can reach speeds of up to thirty-five miles per hour. Their bodies are **streamlined**, and their smooth skin is rubbery to the touch.

▲ *A dolphin's blowhole closes tightly when it is underwater.*

Fish swim by moving their tails and bodies from side to side, but dolphins and whales swim by moving their powerful **tail flukes** up and down. They breathe through a single blowhole in the top of the head, which closes tightly when they are underwater.

To swim efficiently at top speed, dolphins often leap into the air as they swim. This way, they can take a breath without slowing down. Only dolphins, not porpoises, do this "porpoising."

Dolphins have excellent memories, and they can solve problems and invent their own games. They are among the smartest animals on our planet. But their world and brainpower are so different from our own that I think most measures of their "intelligence" may not mean much.

Dolphin Anatomy

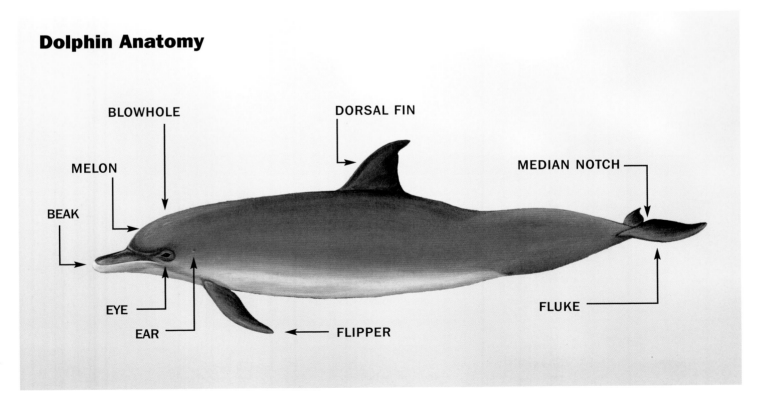

BLOWHOLE

DORSAL FIN

MELON

MEDIAN NOTCH

BEAK

EYE

EAR

FLIPPER

FLUKE

▲ *Two bottlenose dolphins swim gracefully near the water's surface.*

A Confusion of Names

When Is a Porpoise Really a Dolphin?
And When Is a Dolphin Not a Dolphin?

Dolphins, porpoises, and whales together make up a group of mammals called **cetaceans** (pronounced "se-tay-shins"). But the names *whale*, *dolphin*, and *porpoise* cause many problems.

Generally, whales are the biggest cetaceans, while dolphins are small to middle-sized, and porpoises are smaller still.

But it's not quite that simple. Some dolphins are bigger

◄ *Hector's Dolphin*

▲ *Mahimahi, or Dolphinfish*

than the smallest whales. For example, the bottlenose dolphin grows to thirteen feet, whereas the melon-headed whale, which is sometimes called the electra dolphin, reaches only nine feet. And the spectacled porpoise is seven feet larger than several small dolphins, such as the five-foot-long Hector's dolphin.

Also, in some countries, such as the United States and Australia, many people use the word *porpoise* to describe *all* small cetaceans.

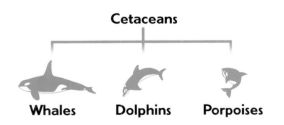

Cetaceans

Whales   Dolphins   Porpoises

▲ *Spinner Dolphins*

The melon-headed whale is one of six "whales," including killer whales and pilot whales, that are really dolphins. More confusingly, these six are often called "blackfish," even though not all are black—and they are mammals, not fish.

Adding to the confusion about names are the mahimahi, large tropical fish that are widely called "dolphins" or "dolphinfish." But they are fish, not mammals.

4

A Variety of Species

There are about eighty **species** of cetaceans. Of these, there are five species of river dolphins, six species of porpoises, and at least thirty-three species of oceanic dolphins, in the family Delphinidae.

The exact number is uncertain. For example, there are many differences in the size, shape, and color of bottlenose dolphins around the world. Coastal bottlenose dolphins are smaller than those living in the open ocean. At present, all bottlenose dolphins are classified as one species, but some scientists think there should be two or three species.

The bottlenose dolphin is so named for its ▶
"bottle-shaped" mouth, which looks like a nose.

Dolphins have sharp, pointed teeth for catching and holding their **prey**, which is usually swallowed whole, headfirst. Their teeth—up to 260 of them—are all the same size and shape. Most dolphins have a distinct beak.

Porpoises are smaller and stouter than most dolphins. Their rounded head has no beak. Their teeth are spade-shaped, for cutting up fish too large to be eaten whole.

The five species of river dolphins are adapted to life in murky river water. Most are highly endangered.

Out of the seventy-seven known species of cetaceans on Earth, ten species are endangered.

A pair of dusky dolphins swim and play in their underwater world. ▶

5

Where They Live

Orcas, the largest of all dolphins, are found in all seas, from the **equator** to polar ice, and from harbors to the open ocean. Other dolphins, such as common and bottlenose dolphins, are also widespread through most seas. Many dolphins roam the open ocean, searching for schooling fish and squid. But some live in just one river or **estuary**, or along a particular coastline.

Some, such as Fraser's dolphins, live only in the **tropics**; others, such as right whale dolphins, are found only in cool water.

River dolphins live in large rivers such as the Yangtze, in China, and the Amazon, in South America. Several other species often live in fresh water, too. Some of these species travel freely between sea and river, but often there are separate groups that seem to live only in rivers and estuaries. The finless porpoise in the Yangtze River, and tucuxis in the Amazon and Orinoco rivers of South America are among these groups.

The Hector's dolphin lives only around the New Zealand coastline, nearly always within six miles of the shore. It is often found in shallow water off sandy beaches, where it enjoys playing in the breaking waves. With a population of about 3,500, it is the rarest marine dolphin in the world. The adult Hector's dolphin is normally about four feet long, making it one of the smallest dolphins on Earth.

Some of the river dolphins are much rarer. With fewer than fifty individuals left, the Yangtze River dolphin will probably be **extinct** soon.

▼ *Hector's Dolphins*

Maui, a bottlenose dolphin, plays "seaweed games" with a diver. ▲

6

Their Underwater Families

Most dolphins live in groups called **schools** or **pods**. Oceanic dolphins live in small, stable groups that come together in large, temporary clusters, often of many thousands. Their **diet** consists of squid and fish, which are sometimes found in big schools, too, but are widely scattered across the ocean. Large groups of dolphins have a better chance of finding food than one animal or a small group of animals.

Once their prey is found, a large group of dolphins working together can easily herd the **quarry**, with the dolphins taking turns to rush in

NOTES

There are many stories of lone dolphins from around the world, dolphins that have left their own kind and sought the company of humans. Most of these loners are bottlenose dolphins. This is "Maui." During the 1990s she played with swimmers off Kaikoura, New Zealand. Maui loved "seaweed games." She has since moved back into bottlenose society.

▲ *A small pod of bottlenose dolphins "bow rides" in front of a moving motor vessel.*

and feed on the fish. The group also provides protection from **predators** such as orcas and sharks.

Another advantage of living in family groups is the ability to care for young or injured members. If a dolphin is injured, other dolphins will often help by supporting it at the surface so it can breathe. A tragic result of these strong bonds within a group, however, is mass strandings.

Food supplies are more predictable around coastlines and in estuaries, so dolphins living there do not need to travel very far, and they live in smaller groups. River dolphins live by themselves, or in small groups.

7

Their Never-ending Search for Food

Fish for Breakfast, Lunch, and Dinner

Dolphins and porpoises are hunters that **prey** on a wide variety of squid and small, schooling fish such as herrings and sardines. They work together in groups to capture their prey, circling around a school of fish, or diving below a school to herd the fish to the surface. Bottlenose dolphins sometimes slide up onto riverbanks to catch the fish they are chasing.

Dolphins use **echolocation** when they are hunting. They send out beams of high-pitched clicks that bounce off objects

Common dolphins, gannets, and other ▸ seabirds follow a fast-moving school of fish.

such as fish or the seafloor. The returning sound, or echo, tells the dolphin the size, shape, and location of the object—a "sound picture." River dolphins live in murky water and need echolocation both to find their way around and to find their food.

Dusky dolphins are very acrobatic. Their leaps and tail slaps are used to announce, "I've found fish!" and to herd the fish. Sometimes these leaps and slaps are also part of **mating** behavior, or simply for fun.

◀ *An orca carries a stingray around before eating it.*

NOTES

As top predators in the sea, orcas have the most varied menu of all dolphins—including at least twenty species of cetaceans. Luckily, they don't eat divers or photographers!

21

8

How They Keep in Touch

Dolphins have a lot of fun. Play is common among the young of most mammals, but usually adults play much less. Among dolphins and whales, the adults play, too.

Dolphins speed alongside boats, surf on waves, or ride the bows of boats or whales. They jump and chase, invent games, and play with fish, bits of seaweed, driftwood, feathers, or anything else they can find. They play with other kinds of dolphins and with people. Porpoises lack the playfulness of dolphins, and they usually avoid people.

Dolphins have good eyesight, a keen sense of touch, and excellent hearing. They make many noises, such as clicks, whistles, squeaks, and barks, which they use to **communicate** with each other.

NOTES

Dolphins love seaweed games. I met these two dusky dolphins a long way from the shore. They probably had picked up this piece of seaweed close to shore and carried it around with them.

Touch is very important to dolphins, not just in courtship, but every day. They often nudge or stroke each other with their flippers or tails. Males often argue over "who's in charge" by slapping their tails, clapping their jaws, and even ramming or biting each other.

Dolphins use behaviors such as tail slaps and leaping out of the water to communicate with other dolphins, as part of cooperative feeding behavior, and often simply for fun.

▾ *Dolphins, like this pair, are far more playful than their porpoise "cousins."*

9

The Circle of Life

Larger animals usually live longer than smaller ones. The small harbor porpoises live up to fifteen years. Most dolphins live at least twenty-five years, and sometimes forty to fifty years. Pilot whales can live up to sixty years, and orcas stay alive up to ninety years.

Normally only one **calf** is born at a time. Birth takes place underwater and can take up to a few hours. The calves are born tailfirst. If they were born headfirst, they would not be able to breathe until they were free from their mother, and therefore might drown.

Another female, a "midwife" or "aunt," often helps the newborn calf to the surface of the water, where it takes its first breath. The calf is looked after and nursed for about a year. The mother's rich milk is pumped into the calf's mouth.

Diseases, injuries, strandings, and predators, such as sharks and orcas, take their toll on dolphin populations—so do humans. They are also accidentally caught in fishing nets, hit by boats, and weakened or killed by pollution.

◄ *A calf and its mother are inseparable for the first year of the newborn's life.*

10

Killer Whales and Pilot Whales

Although they are much larger than the smallest whales, orcas, or killer whales, and pilot whales belong to the dolphin group.

The largest of all dolphins, orcas grow to a weight of ten tons and a length of thirty-two feet. Their diet includes several

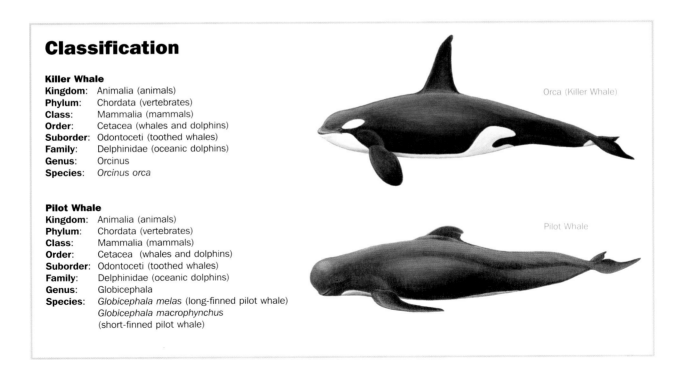

Classification

Killer Whale
Kingdom: Animalia (animals)
Phylum: Chordata (vertebrates)
Class: Mammalia (mammals)
Order: Cetacea (whales and dolphins)
Suborder: Odontoceti (toothed whales)
Family: Delphinidae (oceanic dolphins)
Genus: Orcinus
Species: *Orcinus orca*

Pilot Whale
Kingdom: Animalia (animals)
Phylum: Chordata (vertebrates)
Class: Mammalia (mammals)
Order: Cetacea (whales and dolphins)
Suborder: Odontoceti (toothed whales)
Family: Delphinidae (oceanic dolphins)
Genus: Globicephala
Species: *Globicephala melas* (long-finned pilot whale)
Globicephala macrophynchus
(short-finned pilot whale)

Orca (Killer Whale)

Pilot Whale

▲ *Pilot whales*

hundred species of animals, including whales, porpoises, dolphins, seals, sea lions, fish, sharks, squid, penguins and other seabirds, and even turtles! Orcas are perhaps the ocean's "ultimate predator"—they are big, fast, and highly intelligent, and they are cooperative hunters, much like wolves are on land.

There are two kinds of pilot whales: short-finned, which are found in warm waters, and long-finned, which live in cool waters. Pilot whales sometimes strand, especially in large, shallow bays where their navigational aids let them down. Their strong instinct to help other whales in trouble means that, unless a large number of the stranded whales can be refloated at the same time, the entire group is doomed.

NOTES

These three orcas are "spyhopping"— raising themselves up vertically out of the water to get a good look around. Orcas use this technique regularly in Antarctica to check out the "menu" for breakfast or lunch up on top of the floating sea ice.

11

Dolphins and People

A Special Connection

Many dolphins like humans. The bottlenose dolphin is the friendliest, but at least ten other species seem to like us, too. There are many true stories of dolphins helping people in trouble: protecting them from sharks, keeping them afloat, and helping them get back to their boats or to shore. There is not a single recorded case of dolphins harming people.

Many people like dolphins, too. Stories of special friendships between humans and dolphins have been around for 2,000 years. Ancient Greeks and Romans thought that harming a dolphin was as wrong as harming a person. Today, many people work to save whales and dolphins, and to protect the seas they live in. But fishermen in some countries hunt them for food. Over the past forty years, tuna fishing nets have killed up to 12 million dolphins. Many die in other kinds of fishing nets. Dolphins are caught for display in marine parks, where half of them die within two years.

People **pollute** the seas with garbage and chemicals, which weaken and kill many dolphins. And people overfish the oceans, depriving dolphins of their source of food.

The future of these magnificent creatures depends largely on us—you and me. All of us.

▼ *A dolphin flicks water at a diver in a gesture of playfulness.*

THE DOMINIE WORLD OF
OCEAN LIFE
ANTARCTICA

Glossary

Calf: A young animal

Cetaceans: Large aquatic mammals that have a streamlined body; a group of mammals made up of dolphins, porpoises, and whales

Communicate: To share information; to send a signal

Diet: The food that an animal or a person usually eats

Echolocation: A means of locating objects by using sound

Equator: An imaginary line circling the Earth and dividing the planet into the northern and southern hemispheres

Estuary: A coastal area where seawater mixes with fresh water from rivers; the tidal area of the lower part of a river

Extinct: To gradually disappear due to diminishing numbers

Mammals: A class of warm-blooded animals in which the female feeds the young with its own milk

Mating: Joining with another animal in order to produce offspring

Pods: Small groups of marine animals of a single type

Pollute: To contaminate or poison

Predators: Animals that hunt, catch, and eat other animals

Prey (n): Animals that are hunted and eaten by other animals

Prey (v): To stalk, or hunt, an animal or group of animals

Quarry: An animal that is hunted by something or someone

Schools: Groups of marine animals of a single type

Species: Types of animals that have some physical characteristics in common

Streamlined: Designed to move very quickly and gracefully

Tail Flukes: The part of a whale or dolphin's tail used to propel the animal through the water

Tropics: Areas of land and sea that are very warm and humid throughout the year